OH MONTY!

...loyd   Nici Gregory

PAVILION

First published in the United Kingdom in 2021 by
Pavilion Children's Books
43 Great Ormond Street
London WC1N 3HZ

An imprint of Pavilion Books Company Limited

Text © Susannah Lloyd, 2021
Illustrations © Nici Gregory, 2021
The moral rights of the author and illustrator have been asserted

Publisher: Neil Dunnicliffe
Editor: Martha Owen
Designer: Sarah Crookes

ISBN: 9781843654964

A CIP catalogue record for this book is available from the British Library.

10 9 8 7 6 5 4 3 2 1

Reproduction by Rival Colour Ltd, UK
Printed by Toppan Leefung Ltd, China

This book can be ordered directly from the publisher online at
www.pavilionbooks.com, or try your local bookshop.

MIX
Paper from
responsible sources
FSC
www.fsc.org   FSC® C104723

Coo-eee! Tiddles?
Oh, there you are.

And Monty,
my *darling* handsome puss.

I have the most **marvellous** thing to show you!
Would you like to see it? You would?

There. Doesn't it look **lovely?**
Extra chocolate *and* bonbons.
Delicious!

I just need to leave it here for a moment.
You **will** look after it,
and **make sure no one eats it**, won't you?

What **delightful** pusscats you are.
I just *knew* I could count on you.

Well, I'll be going then.

Bye now!

Tiddles?
Monty dearest?
I'm back!

Great heavens!
But how can this be?

monty...?

...Did **YOU** see who took the cake?

You didn't? Oh dearie, dearie me.
But *who*? **Who** could it have been?
Whoever can have *done* such a **terrible thing?**

I guess we will
never know.

Now, now, you **mustn't** go upsetting yourself over this, my *darling* Monty. You know you have such *delicate* nerves...

Well, there is nothing for it.
I suppose I will just have to bake another one.

One more cake, coming up!

But please, you really **must** watch it this time.
And that means **you** too, Tiddles.

Poor *dear* Monty can't be expected to look after this cake all by himself you know.

Bye bye, my darlings!

I'm back!

But, oh!
My beautiful cake!

Tiddles!
So it was YOU
all along! I *knew* it!

Out you go, you
naughty puss!

And look!

You've upset poor *darling* Monty too!

No, you mustn't blame yourself, *dear sweet* Monty. I'm sure there was nothing more you could have done to stop her.

Oh Monty, my *darling*, however can I make it up to you?
I know! A nice slice of cake!

After all,
you *do* deserve it...